A MAN OF HONOR

A Marlowe And

LAPD Officer Agnes Graham Mystery

September 1942

A Novella

by

gay toltl kinman

Editing & Proofreading by William R. Kinman
Cover designed by Peggie Chan
Photo of gay toltl kinman by Brian and Lilly Loo Studios

Published in the United States of America
By Mysterious Women

Also by gay toltl kinman

MYSTERY NOVELS

Death in A Small Town
Death in Covent Garden
Upclose and Personal
Death in Rancho Las Amigas
Wolf Castle (originally published as Castle Reiner)
Murder and Mayhem at The Huntington Library
Death in Hamburg
Death in...

CHILDREN'S MYSTERIES

The Adventures of Lauren Macphearson
Lauren Macphearson and The Scottish Adventure
Lauren Macphearson and The Colorado Adventure
Lauren Macphearson and The Jumbled Cupboard Adventure
Lauren Macphearson and The Ghostly Adventure

Super Sleuth: Five Alison Leigh Powers Mysteries
The Mystery of The Missing Arabian
The Mystery of The Missing Miniature Books
The Mystery of The Octagon House
The Secret of The Equestrian Park
The Secret of The Strange Staircase

Gilly's Divorce or Don't Make The Mistakes I Did

NON-FICTION

Desserticide II: AKA Just Desserts and Deathly Advice
Gilly's Manual and Advice on Coping with Your Divorce

PLAYS

The Play's The Thing: A Collection of Plays
A Little Theater Mystery
Death In Russia
Putting Mother's Seat Belt On
Revenge
The Audition
The Mystery Writer
The Thief
Wicked Well
The Purloined Letter
Not One More Word
The Ashes of Zane Grey
Baskets to Jade
Esther Howland: Queen Of Hearts
(A Ten-Minute Biographical Play)
Esther Howland: Queen Of Hearts
(A One-Act Biographical Play)
Nicholas Owen: Builder Of Secret Places
(A Ten-Minute Biographical Play)
Nicholas Owen: Finder Of Secret Places
(A One-Act Biographical Play)
Home Sweet Murder
Mr. Marshall's Doppelganger
The Deposition
Unscheduled Changeover in Hamburg 1974

Deaths in Hollywood 1942:
The Marlowe and LAPD Officer Agnes Graham Series

Neither Tarnished Nor Afraid (a short story) in <u>Murder on Sunset Boulevard</u> (A Sisters in Crime / Los Angeles anthology). Set in July 1942. Top Publications 2002.

Mean Streets (a short story). Set in August 1942. Mysterious Women 2012.

A Man of Honor (a novella). Set in September 1942. Mysterious Women 2016.

A MAN OF HONOR

LAPD Officer Agnes Graham is patrolling Hollywood Boulevard when her PI friend Marlowe invites her for an evening on the off-shore gambling ship, the *SS Rex*. He needs her to help him in his investigation. He has been hired by a Hollywood movie studio to find out who is harassing their popular star. Then someone dies in a bathtub. Suicide? Accident? Murder? Now the investigation takes a new turn.

September 1942

Friday. I had the Hollywood beat, Vine and Sunset, and I was just an hour into my noon shift and hot. Most of the rowdies were drunken servicemen, but the real crime came from pickpockets. As I kept my eye out for them, Marlowe drove his car to the curb in front of me.

"You're illegally parked, sir," I said.

"Got an ice cold Coca Cola here." He waved the bottle. "Can I bribe you with that, officer?"

September is our hottest month and today proved it.

I got in, took the bottle and felt the icy, sweet, tingling liquid flow down my dry throat. About two seconds later I handed the empty bottle back to him.

"Got an assignment for you for tomorrow night," he said.

"I'm off."

"That's why you're coming with me, Graham."

"What's the assignment?"

"We're going to the *SS Rex* and do a little gambling."

I looked at Marlowe. "Why do you need me?"

"Somebody might recognize me. I want it to look like I'm just out on a date having fun. But my date has to be working, too—eyes and ears open, observing. If I call you an endearment, don't shoot."

I guffawed. When we'd first met, he had called me 'sweetheart' and I'd promised to shoot his manhood off if he did it again—even though he was my father's friend.

"Depends—got another coke?"

He gave me a second full bottle just as cold as the first one.

"I take my gun?"

He nodded. "Before you say you don't have anything to wear, it's for working stiffs, so whatever dress or skirt and blouse you have in your closet will do."

Actually, that was my next question, but drinking the coke had slowed me down. He handed me a flyer. I read:

Play Outside the 3 mile limit.

Park at the pier at the end of Colorado Avenue Santa Monica.

Follow the X to the SS Rex.

Open for play—24 hours a day.

Dine and Dance to the Rhythm of the Rex Mariners.

More about food, racing results, and other alluring information that ended with:

The World's Largest Ship Casino! Anchored in calm waters off

Santa Monica pier.

"Dining and dancing not included in this trip," Marlowe said, "but I'll spring for the twenty-five cent round-trip on the water taxi."

"That would be 'an enjoyable twelve-minute boat ride.'" I read from the flyer.

"Yep."

When he picked me up at seven on Saturday, he said, "I've got some chips for you to gamble with. Take your time, try to make them last as long as you can. Have you played roulette before?"

I laughed. "Never been to a den of iniquity before." That's what some politicians and law enforcement-types were saying about the *SS Rex*. Big political football, careers could rise and fall on it, I'd heard. People didn't agree about the evils of the *Rex,* including the working stiffs, as Marlowe called them, and even famous folk. From one to three thousand people went there every twenty-four hours. At least that's what the owner, who called himself the Commodore, claimed. And it took in $300,000 a day. No gambling allowed in California, but the *SS Rex* was outside the California state boundary line, the three-mile limit, and had it all—slot machines, card games, craps.

Maybe people wanted something different and the *Rex* offered it. A little bit of excitement, danger, the idea of doing something risqué.

The twelve-minute ride over was a blur, the water taxi loaded to the gunnels with anxious people. I was taking it all in, not really thinking like a police officer, which I should have been doing all the way. I was caught up in the excitement of something different, too, something that I, Agnes Graham, would never do—go to a gambling ship.

The taxi emptied quickly. Marlowe let the herd go ahead. They seemed to be in more of a hurry than we were. Once aboard, if one can say that of a ship that had inoperable engines, Marlowe, hand on my elbow like a true gentleman, steered me through the gambling rooms. I tried to look nonchalant, as though I did this every night and sometimes before breakfast, but it was hard not to gawk like the tourist I was. Shucks, like the hick I was.

He guided me to the back of the last large room and to one of the roulette tables. A miasma of cigarette and cigar smoke choked me. Other smells too—whiskey, sweat, anxiety, fear, hope and despair. Not really all the latter, but it was on the faces of those at the table.

He told me in a whisper that the hallway, a few feet away, led to the private gambling rooms where the high rollers, special guests and other hoity-toity, played. He didn't exactly use all those words but that was the impression I got.

At the table, Marlowe pulled out a stack of chips and set them in front of me. I studied the table. Did I want black or red, *noir* or *rouge*, and what number. I thought to play the same number and color, maybe every third turn of the wheel. Make the chips last longer, as Marlowe had suggested.

Marlowe stayed most of the time. I guessed he was keeping up his 'date' cover by not leaving me alone for long, but he did take short forays away. Each time he returned, he made comments to whoever was standing next to him, and to me—but no business talk between us. The gamblers were men mostly. Maybe the women were at the slot machines, roulette being more of a man's game. Those were my idle thoughts while I studied, without being obvious, those around me. Some of the men still wore their hats, much like the rail crowd at the Santa Anita Race Track.

Deep-cleaved young and pretty women selling cigarettes and cigars moved among the crowded tables. The matches and view were free.

Glancing around I recognized a couple of LAPD cops, obviously not on duty, and a pickpocket from Hollywood Boulevard. He looked like he was trying to get rid of whatever he'd 'earned' that day. Maybe that's why he was a pickpocket, what better way to support his habit? I debated about keeping an eye on him but decided to concentrate on our mission. I'd catch him next time he was in Hollywood.

The other thing I noticed was the silence. Oh, there was noise and background music, hit tunes, some of which I recognized from hearing the records played a lot, but I wasn't into music. I just noticed the absence of people talking. And the eyes of the gamblers. I thought back to the boat ride here. Everyone seemed to have dead eyes. No conversations. Not natural. I felt a little shiver.

No wonder the cost of the ride was round trip. I didn't think some of those at the roulette table would have any money to get back to the Santa Monica pier.

Across the room was the first class restaurant, with cuisine by Henri—that was also touted on the flyer. Later we saw women in long dresses and men in evening clothes on their way to and from the restaurant.

They looked a lot fancier than the working stiffs at the gambling tables, I didn't know what Marlowe's case was. He only told me what I needed to know.

Then—my number came up. Red Seven. A pile of chips was pushed my way, about three times what I had started with. Even Marlowe looked surprised.

"That's about a thousand. Good work Graham."

A thousand! That meant Marlowe had started me off with about three hundred. That was quite a stake. "Do you want it? I owe you."

"Never touch the stuff." Marlowe hadn't gambled at all. All the better to observe—what, I didn't know. Marlowe told me to gather the chips and we went to the lounge. He ordered bourbon, and the waitress named the brands available. Definitely a classy joint. Then he said, "And the lady will have a glass of—"

"Beer," I said which set the waitress reciting another list of brands. Can't say there weren't any choices. Then I remembered that the Commodore had been liquor smuggling during prohibition.

"Got your gun handy?" Marlowe whispered a few minutes later when he leaned closer.

I nodded. My purse was on my lap. I'd just had a swig of beer. Not a good idea to be drinking and shooting. I noticed Marlowe hadn't touched his drink.

Several thoughts skittered around in my brain—a shoot-out amidst all these people? Nope. A heist—steal the money from the counting room? Or something not related to the gambling?

Marlowe lit another cigarette. He put the glass to his lips, but didn't drink. I wondered if he was accidently going to knock it over or pour it into some plant.

Nix on the plants, none around.

"What are we waiting for?"

"Midnight."

"Midnight!"

"You don't have to go into work until noon tomorrow."

Before I could give him a smart mouth response, he jumped up. "Now. We're on."

Then I saw her. Lorna Doone.

Wearing a long white dress that glowed as though a spotlight was on her. She came out of the hallway that led to the private gambling rooms near where I had been playing roulette. She staggered and seemed slightly dazed. Drunk? She looked pale, on the side of ill. She reached out to touch the wall as if to steady herself. Marlowe was instantly at her side. It took me a few minutes to get my sea legs for the ship seemed to be rocking. Before I could move, a man rushed over to them. He looked very concerned and took her pulse. I knew the *Rex* boasted of a full-time medical doctor aboard, perhaps this was him.

Then an explosion of light. Flash bulbs. I was blinded and plunked back down in the chair. Photographers. Taking her picture. Ironically, at the first flash she perked up. Like an old war horse at the starting gate bell. But she was by no means old. She flashed right back at them—her famous smile and posed, waving to the crowd. Her luxuriant red curly hair instantly recognizable. Marlowe stepped back, out of the cameras' frame. He dragged the doctor with him.

If the photographers thought they were going to catch her in less than her glamorous Hollywood self, they were wrong.

It had been a set-up, I thought. Marlowe knew what was going to happen. And he had to have a woman along, namely me, to help get Miss Doone out of here.

Where was her escort? Had she come alone? Why? A gambler? A lot were around. I was sure I'd find the answers to all those questions, but not right now. Marlowe needed a little help, so I sprang forward as sprightly as I could but it was more like a lurch.

Five photographers. What a coincidence. Four newspapers in Los Angeles but the other one could be from Santa Monica. The boys soon spread out, looking around for other stars or famous people. They might even discover the bar. In fact, Marlowe seemed to be arranging something with our waitress as he was giving her money and pointing to the photographers. He had Miss Doone by the arm. I took the other side.

"Let's get you to the ladies room," I said. Now she was sagging. We got in there none too soon. Whatever she'd had for the past few meals, she had no longer.

"So sick," she mumbled.

"We're getting out of here, back to dry land. Put on my jacket." It was black and would cover the low-cut white dress that made her stand out. Marlowe was waiting for us. We headed for the water taxi platform. The little boat was bobbing and that seemed to bring up a few more meals from Miss Doone. I bet she was about to throw up the rhinestone clips on her *peau de soie* high heels. We were handling a partially comatose person, not that she weighed a lot.

A few people got on the taxi, not as many as coming out here, but they were in their own world, curious about her, but not quite awake or sober. Or maybe stunned that they hadn't won bags of money.

The twelve-minute ride was an eternity. At the pier, Marlowe got one of the cabs to take us to his car. Even though it wasn't a long walk, she never would have made it. And we would have had a hard time trying to drag her. Dead weight is dead weight. We had to wait for a few more hors d'ocuvres to puddle on the ground, luckily missing all of our shoes.

"We should take her to the hospital," I said.

"There's a place nearby. I told the good doctor on board that we would escort her to a medical facility."

"So that was the ship's doctor?"

"Hard to get rid of him. Luckily someone pulled him away on another emergency, a man having a heart attack while losing in a poker game."

I wondered if Marlowe had arranged that, too. And, if so, why he wanted to get rid of the doctor. Seemed that man could have helped her. No time for those thoughts now.

"Where—" I started to ask.

"A specialist," Marlowe said.

The 'place nearby' turned out to be a Studio doctor's house. He was ready for us, a nurse in uniform at his side. Of course, Marlowe had planned ahead. I was greatly relieved that Miss Doone was now getting professional care. Nursing is not one of my finer talents.

We left and headed back to Hollywood and my home in Silverlake. "Marlowe, what's going on?" I asked once we got on the road. "You knew about the photographers and about Miss Doone and what was going to happen."

"Let's just say I had the same tip those guys did. Only we were lucky. The police were supposed to raid the ship, that's what the pictures were going to be about. Particularly about our star being arrested. Drunk and disorderly. That was another tip."

"I'd love to have seen her throwing up all over the arresting officers." I gave a good guffaw at that mental scene.

"The other tip was that someone was going to give her something to knock her out. Plus the tipster hinted that maybe she's pregnant."

"What! But her husband is—-"

"Very astute, Graham. Next you'll be counting the months on your fingers. Yes, there has been a little extra-curricular activity with her current leading man."

"Gosh darn She's the last person—"

"That's exactly why someone set this up."

"Someone who?"

"Good question, Graham. Who has the most to gain? What would this do to Miss Doone's career now that she's about to star in an epic Pollyanna-type picture?"

"She'd be out. Contract cancelled. Isn't there some sort of morals clause—?"

"Yep. There's someone who is lobbying very strongly for the part, makes no secret she wants it."

"I don't know much about Hollywood insider information. You're going to have to tell me or leave me in suspense."

"Ah, Graham, you're right There is a world outside of Hollywood intrigue and gossip. The person I'm talking about is Kirsta Black. And her mother is the ultimate stage mother. She lives her life through her daughter."

"The type who would do *anything* to further her daughter's career?"

"Yep."

"Wasn't she in silent films years ago?" I was dredging up some miscellaneous information in my mental trivia file.

"The very same."

"Harassment of Miss Doone is our case. Small irritating incidents have occurred on the set, but what happened tonight and what was supposed to happen—that's why I was hired."

"That's your case? Who hired you?"

"Morgan Productions. Big Jim didn't like the way things were going." Marlowe chuckled. "He didn't want his star to be skittish about what was going to happen next and she was getting very nervous."

"What—"

"I won't go into details, minor sabotage, like salt instead of sugar, vinegar instead of water. It was getting to her. Big Jim didn't want anything to affect her acting. Then the tip—a lot bigger than what's been happening. Plus as you mentioned there's a moral turpitude clause in her contract, just like everyone else's. If she steps out of line—being drunk on a gambling ship might do it. Plus one word to the wrong person—like Louella—and Miss Doone could be fired. The person to step into her shoes might be Kirsta. Kirsta is good, but she doesn't have the presence Miss Doone has. Or the experience. Kirsta is aiming for the next big picture Miss Doone was cast in."

I compared the two mentally, and had to agree. I yawned. I looked around. Not many people on the road at this hour and sometimes it was just Marlowe's car headlights in the dark. When we arrived at my Queen Anne cottage in Silverlake, he bid me 'good night.' I yawned him one in return, went in and slept the sleep of the dead.

Sunday at noon I reported for duty at the Hollywood Station, still yawning. Mouth opened, I heard the news that woke me up instantly. Kirsta Black had been found dead in her Santa Monica beach house in her bathtub. Some details, but nothing saying suicide, accident—or even murder. Had to be accident.

On my dinner break at 5, I called Marlowe from a pay phone. I wanted to talk about Kirsta's death, what it meant to his case. And of course I wanted to know how Miss Doone was feeling.

He started with Miss Doone first, sort of ignoring my other questions. Marlowe told me, "Miss Doone ingested something. Whatever it was, she's allergic to it and that's what made her sick. And good thing, too, otherwise it might have killed her. Nobody knows what somebody gave her—poison, knock-out drops or what. The other news, and this is for your ears only, is that the fetus was expunged. In other words, her body rejected everything. But she'll be all right."

"Kirsta—"

"They're doing the autopsy. Won't know anything for sure until the report's in. So let's leave our speculations in abeyance for now."

Sometimes Marlowe used some high-flautin' words to get his point across.

"Abeyance, right. So what's next Marlowe?" I had questions, including ones about the fetus, but the phone booth was stifling with the door closed. Traffic and people noise on Hollywood Boulevard were too loud to leave it open.

"Finding out who else was in the private room on the *Rex* to give Miss Doone something and interview them all. The Commodore was most accommodating about providing names of those in the card game and the waiters."

"I'll pick you up at midnight when your shift ends. We should take a look at Kirsta's cottage."

Not long past midnight we arrived at Kirsta's beach house. Definitely not a Marion Davies mansion on the sand in Santa Monica. Just a small wooden cottage that had been built, along with several dozen others, for families to spend the summer at the beach. Not designed for year-round living.

Marlowe had the key given to him by his client, Big Jim Morgan. His studio was paying the rent.

We headed for the bathroom. The claw foot tub sat lengthwise under the frosted glass window, separated from the toilet on the left in the corner by a curtain, a pink flowery thing.

She was found with her head at that end by the curtain. The taps were at the other end. On the right stood a small dressing or vanity table, plain pink fabric skirt flowing from the edges to the floor. A profusion of cosmetics on the top, *Evening in Paris* perfume and Pond's Cold Cream, on the gold filigreed tray. A triptych mirror and a small kidney-shaped seat dressed with the same pink fabric completed the ensemble. To the right of that, against the adjoining wall, was a clothes hamper and on the back of the door hung a robe and night gown. Pretty, frothy, feminine—and see-through. More for company entertaining, I thought, than keeping warm during the chilly nights here at the beach.

A dainty wastepaper basket sat in the corner on the other side of the door against the last wall, not far from the sink with a mirrored cabinet above that reflected the triptych mirror of the vanity table.

I imagined the scene—her head against the small pillow attached to the rim of the tub. Perfect for soaking.

"What I want you to tell me is if she got into the tub on her own or was placed there."

"What!" I looked at him. "You're thinking she was—"

"Not thinking anything, just covering all bases. So give me your take. Maybe you can tell. You're a woman. What would you look for?"

I had to think. "If she was taking a bath—bathmat, slippers or shoes by it. The night gown and robe are several feet away, hanging up on the back of the door. Otherwise some clothes, underwear, at least. Maybe put the things on the vanity chair, maybe move it within easy reach." None of that was there now but it could have been taken away, moved by Momma who found her or the officials who took the body away. Over the rim of the tub was a typical wire basket with a large sponge, back brush and a bar of soap. I saw the towel rack on the wall between the tub and the vanity. Not that far, really. Stand up in the tub, reach for it. Marlowe followed my eyes, and probably my thoughts.

"Anything else?"

I shook my head. Frances, my father's elegant wife, would have been the person to ask about frou frou in the bath, not me. I was strictly utilitarian.

Someone in the cottages across the walkway might have seen the light on. In fact, I could see a light across the way through the frosted glass. Two thirty in the morning and someone was up.

"Let's go talk to her neighbors."

Outside, I could smell the briny, fishy aroma from the water three rows of similar cottages away. A narrow walkway separated the blocks of cottages, not wide enough for a car, only pedestrians, bikes and the surrey-fringed pedal machine that every visitor rented at least once.

I knocked on the door of the lighted cottage. Marlowe went around the other side where there was another lit window.

It's always a surprise to be greeted by a stereotype. But there he was—hairy chest covered barely by an undershirt, once white, with evidence of a red sauce and sprinkles of cigarette ash. He told me his name was Stanley.

I introduced myself, leaving off the 'Officer' since I wasn't on duty, nor in my jurisdiction. "I'm helping to investigate the death of your neighbor Miss—"

"That movie star who lives over there?" He nodded to Kirsta's cottage.

I nodded back. I was trying to phrase my next question delicately but was having a bit of a problem—like when did you see her last through the bathroom window?

"Starkers," he said.

I guess he got the reaction he was hoping for from me because he smirked.

"She opens the bathroom window just before she takes a bath. Window squeaks so loud like she's announcing it to the world. She knows I'm watching. She knows Ed is too." He waved his hand toward the cottage on the other side where Marlowe had gone.

"Um…on a regular basis?"

"At least once a day. Window's always closed otherwise. Can't see through the glass."

"She…um..took a bath when?"

He seemed to be thinking hard about that. Or maybe he was rerunning his mental film of the starkers scene. Then he shook his head. "Saturday, late afternoon, say, about five. Funny thing, they found her in the bath on Sunday, but the window wasn't open." He frowned.

"See anybody over there after that?"

"Nope, but I wasn't here all the time. Been working double shifts. There's a war on donchaknow?"

I got his name. I could figure out what his address was. Wouldn't be hard to get his work information, verify his alibi if that's what Marlowe wanted. I was surprised he wasn't more bowled over by Kirsta-the-star, as opposed to Kirsta-the-starkers-neighbor. Maybe he was tired after working a double shift.

Marlowe came from the other side. He led me past the cottages to the boardwalk on the beach before we said anything. I told him what my guy Stanley had said.

"Talked to Ed, says the same thing. He's been away, just found out about Kirsta being dead. Captain Ladd's men will probably talk to them."

Ladd. All I could think of was Alan. I'd heard he was really short, and had to stand on a box to kiss his leading lady if she was taller than him, and most of them were. He'd have to do that next to my 5'8". But maybe it was just a rumor started by a jealous actor. No matter, I didn't expect to ever be standing next to him—or kissing him!

Marlowe was talking…something about the Santa Monica P.D. "We've got to get a timeframe of what she did and where she went and with whom from when she left the *Rex* on Saturday night to Sunday at eight in the morning when Momma found her. Probably having the bath at night, too early for her in the morning. That goes to opportunity, but we have to narrow down the timeline to find out who can't account for that time. We need to find out what she was doing after she got off the *Rex*. Find out exactly when she left and when she got home. Let's go back to the *Rex* and ask a few questions."

I sighed. Now I was working seven days a week.

"Okay, not tonight," as though he'd read my mind, or my expression. Or maybe it was because I was yawning again.

"Marlowe. Wait." He'd started toward the car. Two a.m. cold, with the sea breeze. I needed a jacket.

He stopped.

"What path are we following? Who slipped Miss Doone something and set her up? Or Kirsta Black's death, which you're talking like it's a possible murder?"

"Need the timeline for Kirsta, see if she connected with Miss Doone at all. That's related to the issue about who gave Miss Doone what on the *Rex*." Marlowe was talking slowing as though I was a toddler. At this point, mentally I was, because I couldn't follow his reasoning.

"We're following the Miss Doone path."

"But Kirsta keeps getting in the way."

Marlowe tugged his ear. "You could say that."

"I just did."

He grinned. "Let's go, Graham, it's cold here."

I trotted along behind him like a doggie at his heels. Were there other apt descriptions of my actions? A lamb to slaughter?

When my shift ended Monday at midnight, and in the wee hours of Tuesday we went back to the *Rex*. I'd had about six hours sleep. Not bad.

On the way there, Marlowe told me about the autopsy. Finally! Kirsta died of hypothermia.

"Makes sense, lying in cold water for a few hours."

Marlowe didn't say anything for a few minutes. I sensed I'd made another gaffe.

"She was murdered," he said.

"What! Why do you say that?"

"Because the water wouldn't get cold enough in the tub to cause that."

"Then how—"

"That's what we're going to find out."

I still had my chips, hadn't cashed them in. Marlowe went off to find out what he could about Miss Doone's visit. My colleagues at the roulette table were not overly talkative as I learned when I tried to strike up a conversation with those on either side of me. They feigned deafness, concentrating on winning back their losses. They weren't here to socialize. Particularly not with someone who looked the opposite of Miss Doone.

Only the man across the table at the same end as me said a few words. I stuck to my original plan of playing only every third spin of the wheel. He didn't play every one either. He had some high priced chips in his hand.

Marlowe had selected this particular roulette table for me—so he could watch the private rooms, as he had that first night. They were close by with the doors open. However, a guard was at the hallway entrance, so not just anyone could saunter in.

I was losing my winnings from last time when Marlowe came to get me.

On the boat back and at the Santa Monica pier, talked with the boatmen who operated the water taxis, and had Kirsta's presence confirmed, as well as arrival and departure times. Hooray for Hollywood—-stars were always noticed. Great help for detective work.

We were back in Santa Monica and in Marlowe's car before we talked about the case. Both cases. Marlowe learned that Kirsta had been in the same card game with Miss Doone, but only for a few hands. She had departed before we arrived. He also learned Kirsta had left in a huff after an abrasive encounter with the Commodore, her current boyfriend.

"The timing isn't right for Kirsta to have put anything in Miss Doone's drink. Besides, Miss Doone was only drinking water then."

Marlowe pulled a cigarette out of his pack. He played with it, a thoughtful expression on his face, as though looking into the future. I was already half dead from the smoke on the *Rex*. Marlowe knew that I liked breathing untainted air. He stuck the ciggie in his mouth, didn't light it, just started the car and we were off—back to my abode in Silverlake in the almost dawn hours of Tuesday morning.

Tuesday, I was on my beat at noon with six hours sleep again, though it hadn't reached my eyelids, which were drooping and my eyes were scratchy. Didn't know how long I could keep up this double life.

A little talk around the station about Kirsta Black and the Commodore. The Commodore had been his own man, steering clear of the Mafia in the whiskey-running operation during Prohibition, and now with his floating gambling casino. He'd only been able to do that because this was the West Coast, not the East Coast where the Mafia was *el supremo*, or whatever the Italian for that was. But there were wolves at the Commodore's door, or perhaps porthole was a better word. The Mafia was expanding its East Coast monopoly and trying to take over here. But the noisiest wolf at the Commodore's port hole was the California Attorney General and the groups that supported him on the issue of not having gambling in California at all, three miles out or not. I wondered why the state didn't just tax him high instead? Ironically, all the controversy just made the Commodore's business better—more alluring for its sinful ways.

I foot patrolled Hollywood and Vine. On my dinner break, I called Marlowe. Another yawn. My hand was hardly big enough to cover it.

"Since the Commodore and Kirsta were seeing each other, was he behind the harassment of Lorna Doone?" I asked.

"Doubt it. Why would he be? More likely it was all engineered by Momma."

"Where is Kirsta's Momma now?"

"At home, sedated, with twenty-four care since she's hysterical over the untimely death of her beautiful and talented movie star daughter."

"Can't blame her for that."

"Theatrical. The newshounds are playing it big.

I yawned again. Good thing Marlowe couldn't see me. I must have made a sound, because Marlowe said. "Call it a night after your shift, Graham. Keep your ear to the ground. Call me tomorrow, maybe before you start your patrol."

Marlowe knew I didn't have a telephone, so I had to use the one at the station, or a phone booth which I was doing now.

Wednesday I called Marlowe at 11:30 from the station before my noon shift. He told me he had learned what the fight between Kirsta and the Commodore was about. "Cigarette girl told me," he said.

I knew which one. She had been working the end where the private rooms were and near my roulette table. She was beautiful, starlet material for sure. Especially with that Grand Canyon cleavage.

"Kirsta wanted the Commodore to get her the part that Miss Doone was slated for. He refused. She wanted him to invest in the epic movie they're going to start filming and then demand she have the leading role."

"What were they going to do about Miss Doone?"

"That wasn't discussed. Likely not a big concern of Kirsta's."

"Did she threaten him with something?"

"A threat wasn't mentioned by my informant, but she couldn't hang around for all the fireworks. And if he wanted to get rid of Kirsta, all he had to do was toss her overboard. Simple. Clean."

I yawned again. Another officer was behind me, clearing his throat as a big hint. "Got to go, Marlowe. Talk to you Code 7."

A theatrical Momma and a simple guy. Something to think about. I yawned again.

Marlowe picked me up. Thursday was my day off from the police department. We went to Kirsta's cottage again. And back to the bathroom.

"You'd think she'd wake up when the water got cold," I said.

"She was drugged. Didn't I mention that?"

"No, you didn't. How am I supposed to help you if you don't give me all the pieces?"

"Yeah, you're right. Just used to working alone."

I bit back a comment. I didn't want him to oust me from the case just because I was highly irritated.

"From your observation, *we* concluded she didn't get into the tub on her own."

"She was literally an olive in the drink."

"Drink…" Marlow marched into the kitchen and opened the top of the icebox. No surprise, no ice left. He pulled out the pan below. Barely a quarter inch of water.

It took me longer than Marlowe to get it. Not enough water for a whole block of ice to have melted. Everything inside—not that there was that much—was warming up.

"The iceman didn't come," I said.

"The ice went into the drink," Marlowe said. "A block of ice would do it. That was the murder weapon. And she was put in the tub unconscious. Like you pointed out—no bathmat, no slippers. We don't know that she used any of that. But the big clue is that the window was closed. She could have been knocked off anytime after she got home. We don't know what time that was."

"Does Momma know?"

"Captain Ladd's boys will have to take care of getting that information. Momma came in Sunday morning and found her."

"That's about twelve hours after she left the *Rex*. But we don't know what she did in the meantime."

"We have to consider Miss Doone as a suspect. She could have hired someone to get rid of her harasser." Marlowe didn't sound convinced, more like throwing ideas around. I didn't want Miss Doone to be guilty of anything.

"Did Miss Doone know for sure it was Momma doing the harassing?"

"The rumor was everyone knew. Rumor only, Graham. That's why I was hired—to find out who."

I sat down on a kitchen chair. "Was there another man in Kirsta's life besides the Commodore?"

Marlowe took the other chair. He pulled out a cigarette but just played with it, rolling it around in his left hand like a dexterity exercise, because he was right-handed. He tapped it on the table a few times. "Let's look around here, see what we can find. The police have her important papers, address book, whatever she had."

"And we have the leftovers."

"Sometimes leftovers can be better the second day."

"It's past the second day, Marlowe, and everything has spoiled." I pointedly looked at the icebox.

Even though the cottage was small, Kirsta had a lot of personal belongings in it. I couldn't decide whether she was living here permanently or it was just a pied-a-terre, albeit the terre was sand. If she was only here temporarily, like for the summer, no matter that now it was September, then we needed to see her other place, her real home where she lived with Momma.

I had the two bedrooms to search. Both were small. Kirsta's had a three-quarter size bed, dresser, wardrobe in lieu of a closet, chair, and a rag rug. The room seemed smaller than the bathroom.

I looked under and in everything, including pockets, hats and shoes. The free standing wardrobe was full but not crammed. Good clothes. The dresser was packed—silky lingerie, nightgowns, stockings. Potpourri scents arose from each drawer, maybe even *Evening in Paris.*

Of note, was the Whitman's Sampler box full of pictures in one drawer. It still had the aroma of chocolate when I lifted the lid. The pictures seemed recent as though taken during the summer, by the same camera. Kirsta was in some of them, but mostly they were of other young people. One of an older woman in an unflattering bathing suit. Momma? Three of a man who was alone, but the same background of sea and sand. Was this another beau? How did the Commodore fit into all of this, because he sure wasn't in any of the snaps. Just one picture cut out of a newspaper with his name in the caption. Real personal.

The other bedroom seemed to be where Momma stayed when she visited. She definitely didn't live here—only a few pieces of clothing in the wardrobe and the dresser, including the unsuitable bathing suit. So that was Momma in the photograph.

"Marlowe, did you find a camera?" I met him in the kitchen and spread the chocolate aroma pictures on the table.

He shook his head. "Captain Ladd has it."

Marlowe separated out the three pixs of the man alone. "This guy looks familiar. Think he's one of the Commodore's bouncers."

I hoped it was that easy to ID him. "Did you find anything?"

"She didn't eat in much, doesn't read, but has a good collection of records and a nice phonograph."

"All clues to nothing," I said.

"Look at this," Marlowe said as he went into the living room. Marlowe pulled a pair of tweezers out of his coat pocket and carefully pulled something out of the pile of newspapers and magazines. A flyer on pink paper for a rally,

calling people to join the Attorney General's campaign to close down the *Rex.*

Time and date and all the pertinents, but the most interesting thing about it was

the handwritten note at the top.

Kirsta—hope you'll join us.

No signature. Kirsta must have known who it was, or perhaps the flyers

were sent to many people with their name and the same 'personal' note. But I

didn't think so.

"We should talk to Stanley and Ed, see what they know about this." I

started to get up.

"There's something else of interest here." Marlowe used his handkerchief to

pull out a manila envelope, then the script that was inside of it. He showed me

the outside of the envelope. Addressed to Samuel Goldwyn. He turned the

envelope upside down and a note fluttered out. He handed me the tweezers. I

picked up the note.

Kirsta—hope you can show our script to Goldwyn like you said you would.

We love ya. R & D

"Not the same handwriting as the flyer." I said. Marlowe held the envelope

and I dropped the note back in. "Did you read the script?"

"Yep. It's about a famous actress who discovers two unknown script

writers, loves the script, wants to star in it, and takes it to a famous producer.

The movie wins an academy award for best picture and best actress."

"Original," I said.

He put the script back in the envelope and slipped it under the newspapers where it had been. "I'll talk to Ed, you tackle Stanley. Momma might know about the script."

"That kinda stuff—rallies against the *Rex*—that's been going on for a while," Stanley said, looking at the flyer which was now in a file folder protecting any fingerprints. "Trying to organize people. The meetings only tell you all the bad stuff about the *Rex*. Never mention how many jobs people have because of it, or what happens to those people if they close the *Rex* down. Where are they going to get a job?"

"So, you're not a part of this?" I pointed to the flyer again.

"Not me, don't have time for that kind of flag-waving. Don't go out to the *Rex* anyhow. It doesn't have anything for me."

"Do you know who might have written the note?"

He peered at the flyer closely. He shrugged, shook his head. "Could be some young buck just wanted to have a date with her."

"It's not signed."

He shrugged.

"Who's on this committee?" I pointed to the name of it.

He shrugged again.

Marlowe was coming back from Ed's, so I said good-by to Stanley and we went back to Kirsta's. We shared our meager information.

"We need to know more about who's behind the rally. Who organized it? Follow the money."

"Is that what we're going to do next?" I asked, ever the acolyte.

"Nope. Captain Ladd is. He probably already knows all about it since gambling is illegal in the state. We can get what we need from him when the time comes." His voice trailed off as though he had just thought of something.

I wondered why the police hadn't found the rally flyer. Maybe they had, and left it, thinking it wasn't important. Maybe they didn't find it because they were sloppy.

We drove the short distance to the water taxi stop in Santa Monica. The taxis would fill up, standing room only but come back with just a few passengers. I watched while Marlowe showed a boat boy one of the three pictures from Kirsta's to see if he could identify the lone man. The boat boy nodded, then gestured as though explaining something.

He confirmed that Marlowe was right about the bouncer. His name was Andres and he had been assigned by the Commodore to stay with Kirsta while she was onboard the *Rex,* then escort her back and drive her home. Marlowe planned to go to the *Rex* and talk with Andres. He was also planning on talking with the Commodore.

We discussed suspects while driving back. Mine was the Commodore. No matter that I felt Marlowe was right. The way Kirsta was murdered was too sophisticated for a former whiskey smuggler. Heck, maybe he still was. Why bother with time-consuming methods when there were easier ones.

"Got to find out more about her life. Why someone wanted to kill her. I'm going to nose around the studio, see what people thought of her, take a look at her dressing room."

"What about Momma? I'd love to interview her. She must have an opinion."

I expected him to give me a noisy raspberry, but Marlowe was quiet for a moment. "To get her talking, let's give Momma the idea she should sue—don't know who at this point, maybe the Studio. See if we can get her to talk, pull her out of her hysterics because I think she's acting. The spotlight is on her and she's taking full advantage." He sounded more admiring than disparaging of her conduct.

Marlowe then regaled me with some stories about the movies Momma was in. She never made it big, nor made the transition to talkies because of her Polish- Brooklyn accent which she still had and flaunted.

He dropped me off at home. Even though it was early evening, I was thinking beddy-bye time.

On duty the next day at noon. I wanted to go with Marlowe on his interviews at the studio and poke around in her dressing room, and then her house, but I had to settle for working for a living. Marlowe was getting paid for nosing around—I wasn't.

If we could just come up with why she was killed. A nice big fat juicy motive. That motive would have an arrow pointing right to the murderer. Yes, siree, I could solve this one in a flash…if only…

Friday while I was sweating, not glowing as women are supposed to, in the heat in Hollywood, Marlowe interviewed Andres, the bodyguard-bouncer, in cool Santa Monica. I wasn't able to hear the details until my dinner break when I called him from the station. Luckily, Marlowe was in his office.

Andres told him, yeah, he had come back on the water taxi with Miss Kirsta and drove her to her cottage. She hadn't said a word. He knew about the set-to with the Commodore. She was the one who was angry, not the Commodore. He thought the Commodore was ready to dump her after the way she yelled at him. He said he knew the Commodore had liked her, but that didn't mean he felt he had to help her become a star, well, a bigger one because she was already famous.

Marlowe caught me by surprise because he told the next part in Andres' voice, and had me laughing, despite the seriousness of what he said. I'd seen Andres' picture, so I could envision him talking with a slight French accent, a la Maurice Chevalier.

It was also a revelation to hear Marlowe in a different persona, maybe he was a latent actor. Definitely a superb mimic.

"She was spittin' mad. She wanted that part in the movie worse than anything. She had to have someone put money into the movie so she could get the part. The Commodore told her he might as well throw the money overboard. He didn't trust Hollywood. Said they were more crooked than the Mafia. She told the Commodore she could shut the *Rex* down. She said she knew how to do it."

"What did the Commodore do when she said that?" I asked. "Seems to me he'd be ready to throw her overboard at that point."

Marlowe continued in his Andres' voice. "He gave her a look like I hope he never gives me. He was mad, cold, but turned and walked away. Didn't say anything. She was fuming. But I think she got the point it was over between them. She said something like she'd show him." Back in his own voice he related that Andres said goodbye at her front door and went back to the *Rex*.

Although I believed Andres, I had to question his interpretation. It made the Commodore look bad, but I didn't think he was trying to cast any suspicion on his boss. But Andres had taken her home, not realizing he was the last person to admit seeing her alive. That was something to think about.

Marlowe had checked on the time Andres caught the water taxi back. He didn't linger. But killing her would have taken only a few minutes—after he slipped her a mickey. Seemed a stretch.

"Shall I cross him off the list, Marlowe?"

A grunt, which I took as a 'yes.' I wondered how Andres felt about this. He was under orders to escort her home, and now he might be suspected of murder because he was the last to see the victim alive, by his own admission. Scary how fast life—or the lack thereof—changes.

Saturday I was off again, so we went to see Momma at her house in Hollywood. Built well in the 20s, gingerbread style outside, full of dark wood inside, I could move in.

She now knew her daughter's death was murder. Marlowe had convinced her that being calm and candid, telling the truth, might help find her daughter's killer.

"Had to be some jealous son of a bitch. Somebody she wouldn't give the time of day to."

I felt this was a tangent, but I duly wrote down the names of the men Kirsta refused to go out with. "Be seen with," was her mother's phrase.

"And she wasn't engaged to that Commodore, no matter what Louella writes."

"Was she in love with him?" Marlowe asked.

"She was in love with love, with romance, and he was a figure out of an Errol Flynn movie. She thought he could do big things for her. Then when he didn't, she saw him for what he was."

I didn't ask what he was and neither did Marlowe. Maybe he knew.

"Called me Saturday night as soon as she got back from the *Rex* and told me what happened. No financing from him. She said she had another idea and was going to talk to somebody about it. She wanted that picture real bad."

If she talked to Momma after Andres had dropped her off, that took him off the suspect list.

"Who was the person she was going to talk to?" Marlowe asked.

Momma shook her head.

"Did she mean someone she was going to ask for backing or someone she was going to ask for suggestions as to who might do the financing?"

"She didn't say."

"What's your best guess?"

"It was an offhand comment, not like she had a plan. Her plan had been the Commodore all along. She thought she could bring him around to her way of thinking. I thought he'd do it too, as an investment. If she could get the money from someone to invest, then she was in a better position to get the part. She saw it as her big step up."

"What did you think?" Marlowe asked the question. I wanted to know the answer, too.

Momma sighed. "I was trying to figure out the best plan. In the meantime, if she came up with the dough we were set. If she didn't, then I had to do some politicking, call in some favors, do something. I couldn't let my baby just hang out there, not making any progress in her career."

Or Momma's career as a stage mother, I thought.

Marlowe was quiet for a few moments, Momma daubed her eyes with a white lacy handkerchief, I glanced down at my notes.

"Do you think the Commodore killed her?"

"I'd love to say yeah, the son of a bitch did it, but I'd be lying. I don't think he'd be bothered. He's married, you know, keeps it quiet, doesn't live with her anymore. But he doesn't want a divorce. Likes to have his cake and eat it too, know what I mean? If he's married, he can't get married. Get it? Wonder if Louella knows? Well, I'm certainly not going to be the one to tell her. Don't want him looking at me cross-eyed. Don't need those kind of enemies, know what I mean?

I didn't know if Marlowe was getting any leads from all of her talk. His eyes weren't crossed yet, but mine were getting that way. Taking notes wasn't easy.

"Who gave her a script to take to Goldwyn?"

"Oh, those two boys. They were a pair of pests. Live at the beach nearby, wanted her to flog their script around. They had high hopes she would sell it for them. Don't think she did anything. Too many other things going on. Funny, because the only things she reads are scripts. Don't think she read that one. I asked her about it a few times because she said they kept coming around. I wanted to read it, see if it was any good or not. Who knows? But she didn't know where she put it, didn't seem to care if I read it or not. Or if anyone read it."

"So she didn't flog it around?"

Momma was quiet for a moment, her eyes on her hands as she twisted her wet handkerchief. "Not that I know of."

"We need names, Marge. You were closest to her. Who wanted her dead?" He laid it on the line and didn't mince his words, pushing her for some clues. It dawned on me that he talked like he knew her well. Then I remembered all the stories he had told me about her.

"That's what I've been trying to tell you." Tears started streaming down her face. "I don't know who would want to kill my baby."

Marlowe let her cry, which she did silently. A few minutes went by. "Marge, there's got to be somebody mad enough to murder her. She rubbed somebody the wrong way. What about the Commodore's wife?"

Marge shook her head. "She doesn't care what he does. And if she was going to start killing all of his girlfriends, she'd be a busy lady."

"Was Kirsta taking drugs? Didn't pay off whoever she was getting them from? Was she going to turn the person in?" Marlowe fired questions at her.

Marge shook her head at each question as tears continued to run down her face, but she made no sobbing sounds, which was more heartbreaking than a tantrum.

The only solid information we came away with was that Kirsta was alive at eight p.m. on Saturday when she called Momma. No mention of anyone in the cottage or that she was expecting anyone that night.

After the interview, she let Marlowe search Kirsta's room. He was invited, but I wasn't. But Kirsta lived in the whole house, not just her bedroom, so I did a little walk around the living room. It was a trophy room—to Momma. The walls and tops of flat surfaces covered with photos, stills of her with directors and silent screen stars. I recognized some of them—Sennett, Griffith, Pickford, and on and on. She had the attractiveness of youth in the photos, but she wasn't pretty.

I thought about Kirsta. She was pretty and talented. Too bad her personality—from what I knew about her so far— hadn't matched that. It was true you can't have everything.

I wondered where Kirsta's shrine was. Across the hall from the living room was an arched door, wooden and iron-studded in the Spanish style. I guessed it was a den, library, or maybe a small sitting room for the family, leaving the living room as the showpiece for guests. So behind the studded door might be Kirsta's shrine, the place where Momma spent her time—plotting more tricks to throw Miss Doone off her game and out of the running for the next silver screen production. Maybe that was why the door was closed. Now she was going to have time on her hands. She had no daughter to be a stage mother to, no one to live her movie career through vicariously.

"Find anything?" I asked Marlowe when we were in the car.

"Nothing that had the murderer's name on it."

"What did you learn at the Studio?" He hadn't brought me up to date on that.

"Kirsta Black was self-centered, and wanted to be a star with all the trappings—bigger dressing room, best lighting man, best director, best costume designer and her name bigger on the playbills. Not easy to work with is the opinion of most, from gaffers to co-stars, but she was always on time and knew her lines. That goes a long way in Hollywood. She was a professional, everyone agreed on that."

"No motive for murder."

"What we know for sure is that she didn't give Lorna Doone a mickey in her drink because she left the ship even before we arrived."

"But was she responsible, or her mother, for the other harassment?"

"That's true, and Momma wasn't aboard so she couldn't have spiked the drink either," said Marlowe.

"Could have been an accomplice."

"I've got a list of the card players. I'll be interviewing them."

"Remember you had a tip that something was going to happen, so it was planned."

"That bothers me a lot, Graham. I can see the photographers getting it. It's a bigger type of harassment than Momma was doing before. Lorna could have died from the allergic reaction." "You said it was just supposed to knock her out while the place was raided. The raid was cancelled but the Mickey Finn wasn't," I said.

"Two separate actions. The person who slipped her the Mickey Finn did it because the planned raid would bring the photographers there. The second action was because of the first. The first action didn't depend on the second."

"That's deep, Marlowe. I'll have to ponder that when I have time," I said. "Who was the accomplice?"

Marlowe shook his head. "I have a list of names, nobody jumps out. A lot of regulars, I'm told."

"That doesn't eliminate them as a suspect in the Mickey Finn case."

"Mmmm."

"Are we going to do a little more nosing around about her life at the beach?"

"Right, Graham. That's next on our list. I'm going to do some interviewing and you're going to do some patrolling for a few days. And get some sleep."

Marlowe got to do all the sleuthing and I got to do all the working on my paying job. Lots of paperwork and overtime. Things always heated up on the weekends in Hollywood on my beat, so I didn't have the *Rex* or the beach on my mind much. When I went to bed in the early hours of Monday morning, I tried to go over the facts to see if I could come up with something brilliant. I did—a few good hours of sleep.

Monday I was off, and Marlowe had a full day planned. It seemed to me that Marlowe kept focusing on the *Rex*. He felt his answer was there. Not necessarily the murderer. Just the answer that would lead him to the murderer.

When we met for breakfast at Mom's Kitchen, our favorite coffee shop on Hillhurst, Marlowe brought me up to date on the case.

He had interviewed everyone in the card game with Miss Doone, as well as the actress herself. Darn I missed that! She had told him she thought the game was to be a publicity gig. Wardrobe had dressed her to the nines. Publicity was sent out about her trip to the *Rex*. The tie-in was not the Pollyanna epic-type movie in the future—the same one that Kirsta wanted to star in— but one coming out based on a hit Broadway play about a card game.

Marlowe considered that all the people he interviewed were dazzled by her. Added to that was the appearance of the Commodore. He was to pose for publicity shots, supposedly giving her advice about her hand. But the studio photogs never showed up—just the newspaper ones. That was not part of Miss Doone's script.

He told me there were seven people at the table, plus Miss Doone. The Commodore had given them each some $20 chips for participating. Five men and two women. The men remembered the cigarette girl, or rather the protrusions over her tray of wares, but were vague about the waiter. The women remembered both. The waiter was older, not quite the attraction to the women that the cigarette girl was to the gentlemen.

"One of the women remembers the doctor gave Miss Doone a drink, the others don't remember who served the drinks, the waiter presumably, but there was a counter with coffee and some alcohol on it, so they could help themselves. Some were drinking coffee, didn't remember who refilled their cups."

"Where was the doctor when she got sick?" I asked.

"He was in and out of the other rooms. Miss Doone got up, saying she was feeling ill and went into the hallway. Someone went for the doc. He rushed out to help."

"That's when we came in."

Marlowe nodded. "Then someone told him a man was having a heart attack and he went to help him."

"Could someone else have put something in the drink and then the doctor gave it to her, him not knowing?"

"That's where things get interesting. He says he never gave her or anyone a drink. He was drinking ginger ale himself."

We were eating and drinking now, Marlowe puffing away as he told me what he had learned.

"What about Miss Doone? Does she remember who gave her the water?"

"No. She said someone put a glass of water beside her but she doesn't remember who."

"Did she notice that the water had a strange taste?"

He shook his head while shaking another ciggie from the pack.

"Let's say the woman remembers correctly about the doctor giving Miss Doone a drink. Which means he is lying. And if he's lying, he's guilty," I said.

"What's his motive, Graham? He's a doctor. Why would he try to knock someone out?"

I had no answer to that. "Playing devil's advocate, like you do," I smiled. "The woman remembers incorrectly, and the good doctor is telling the truth."

"I checked her out, she seems to be on the up and up."

Then I had another thought. "What about the waiter? Does he remember giving Miss Doone any water? Did he see someone put anything in the water?" I took a breath. I had more questions.

"The waiter doesn't remember serving her water. But there was a pitcher on the counter and it wasn't full afterwards, so others were drinking water. The waiter was looking after five private rooms. So was the doctor."

"I suppose you checked the good doctor out. What did you find out about him?"

"Doc is fifty-three years old. He was associated with the Studio during Momma's heyday there."

"As a doc?" I asked.

"As a first aid person, did a lot of odd jobs. Maybe it paid his way through medical school. After he graduated, he didn't go back to work in the studios."

"So...he knew Momma and obviously, Kirsta. And you. You called her by name, Margery. Do you know her well?"

"I'd met her a few times while working on cases for the Studio. Met Kirsta, too."

Marlowe paid our bill, then we made our way out to the car. I got in and leaned back in the seat. Marlowe knew the players, and things about them I didn't know. He could figure out who wanted Kirsta dead. I felt left out. It was a game and I didn't know all the rules—almost none of them. What good was I to Marlowe? Well—I had helped a little.

I didn't have to ask where he was headed. It would be the *Rex*. He'd tell me in due time what today's agenda was.

"For suspects right now we have Momma, the Commodore, and the doc?" I asked. "Do you have a motive for Momma?"

"Kirsta wasn't doing what Momma told her to do. Maybe Momma didn't want her asking the Commodore for money, it ruined her chances with him. I'm sure Momma didn't want her threatening him."

"Weak, Marlowe."

"Yeah. Can't come up with a motive for her. If she told me she did it, I'd believe her."

"If she told you she didn't, would you believe her?"

He didn't answer that.

"The Commodore had a motive but the murder weapon just doesn't fit his M.O. As for opportunity he could have used his personal launch to get to her place without anyone knowing he was gone from the *Rex*," Marlowe said.

"Do you have any evidence, anybody hint at that?"

"Nope. And that's why we're on our way to interview him."

Oh.

"Continue with our suspect list, Graham."

"The doc is next."

"Don't have a motive for him either," Marlowe said. "He seemed overly concerned when he offered to take care of Miss Doone on the *Rex*, but I chalked that up to the fact that it's his job. And she's a celebrity. If he had given her something and she had the reaction she did, I can see where he might be worried, knowing she was probably having an allergic reaction."

"The only reason we have him on our suspect list is because he could have slipped her a Mickey Finn. Also, he'd know that hypothermia needed ice to make it cold enough."

Marlowe made another 'mmmm' sound.

"What about the neighbors? Would any of them have a motive?"

"Like Stanley and Ed? Think they wanted her alive—to take more baths." He didn't really grin, more of a grimace.

I guffawed, lady that I am.

"Let's go back to the doc."

"What's his motive, Graham?"

"He may have had opportunity, knows Momma and Kirsta... maybe it's something we don't know about."

"We don't know everything, that's for sure."

I thought some more. "His motive could be he's on Momma and Kirsta's side. Maybe he's in love with Kirsta. Or maybe he hates Miss Doone."

"If he was helping Kirsta out, why would he murder her?"

I had nothing to say to that.

"To follow up on your line of reasoning, Graham, maybe something changed. Kirsta threw a few accusations out when she was fighting with the Commodore. What if a guilty party heard that? Even if she or he didn't hear it, between the time she was on the *Rex* to the time she took her fatal bath, she may have tried to blackmail somebody to get the money for the picture's financing. Remember, she wanted that part and it sounds like she was going to do whatever she had to do to get it."

I mulled that over. "But who? Who did she try to get the money from?"

"The murderer. Blackmailing that person for investment money."

"Right back to square one," I said. Actually, we were now in the parking lot for the *Rex* about to have 'an enjoyable twelve-minute ride' to the ship.

The Commodore's office was at the end of the carpeted hallway, past the five private rooms where special card games were played. One wall was a long recessed bookcase. Each shelf had a light that illuminated it, but only three had anything on them. Framed certificates of some kind.

The Commodore sat behind a leather-topped desk. Two chairs in front, and two against the wall next to the door where Marlowe and I stood at that moment. Several feet behind the Commodore and at the end of the bookcase were pale blue velvet drapes pulled over a window, likely a porthole.

The Commodore gestured to the chairs, seat and back padded, covered with leather. Not overly comfortable as I discovered. Maybe he didn't want people staying. I pictured the room being used for interviews of prospective employees, gamblers pleading for a credit extension, that sort of thing. Didn't seem this was the place where he did any real work—signed checks, ordered roulette tables, talked on the telephone, gave dictation to his secretaries. I knew he had his own living quarters elsewhere on the *Rex*.

Idle thoughts, impressions floated around in my mind while we introduced ourselves, or at least me. He and Marlowe knew each other.

The Commodore was handsome. Cary Grant could play him in a movie. I didn't know the story of the one Miss Doone was in, the one that involved a card game. I was willing to bet—maybe a good word here—that it would be set on a ship, and maybe on the *Rex*. Another idle thought while Marlowe started asking questions and I got out the pad and pen to take notes.

The Commodore was quite forthcoming in telling about the tiff—my word—with Kirsta on Friday before her demise.

He seemed innocent, even though I wanted him to be guilty. Everything he said tallied with the cigarette girl's statement and Andres, the bouncer's, aka Kirsta's escort. But differed enough so that it wasn't a verbatim replica, that being the tipoff it had been rehearsed. Yeah, they both worked for the Commodore so they could have collaborated on the story. However, it sounded like the truth to me.

Unfortunately, since I didn't think he was lying, I could flip to the back of my notebook and cross his name off our suspect list.

Damn.

"I told Kirsta I'd dealt with Hollywood before and I'd rather deal with the guys from Chicago. At least I know what they're thinking. She wanted the lead in a picture. Wanted something that would put her up there with Bette Davis, Joan Crawford, and all those stars. All she needed was money. I tried to tell her there was no guarantee the picture would be great." He shook his head and looked down at his clasped hands on the desk.

He was silent for what seemed like a long time. I looked at Marlowe, mentally urging him to ask another question, but he was silent also, looking at the Commodore. Still looking down, the Commodore said, "Whatever character she was playing at the time, and whoever she was supposed to be on the screen, and she acted on the stage, too, that's who she was with me. A different person all the time. She wasn't like any girl I'd ever known. But, after a while, it paled. Too much acting. I didn't know who she was. It was fun at first to be thrown off balance like that, but…" he splayed his hands, palms up in a gesture of resignation. "I couldn't take it anymore. Always performing and I was her audience. That last bout with her, about the money, that was the real her. She was a bitch." Now he held his arms up, in surrender. "I know she's dead. Don't want to speak ill of her, but I'm just telling you the truth. This isn't—" now he waved his hands to encompass the room, and maybe the ship, "Hollywoodland."

"She made a threat," Marlowe stated.

"Yeah." He paused. "She said she could shut the *Rex* down. Don't know what she meant by that. Thought she just said it because she was mad, couldn't think of anything worse to say."

"That threat didn't bother you?"

"Wasn't even sure it was a threat." He paused. "I see what you mean—a reason to kill her. Nope. Didn't kill her. And before you ask, I didn't put a contract out on her either. No reason to. You can believe that or not." He looked defiant. "She's still causing trouble—and she's dead."

Afterwards in Marlowe's car, we sat in the parking lot looking at the lights of the *Rex*, three miles way. Seemed hardly an inch high and two inches long. So small to cause such a big controversy.

"What do you think, Graham?"

"I'm crossing him off our suspect list."

He nodded. "Everything jives with what I've learned. He summed up who she was as good as anyone can. But what did she know that would shut down the *Rex*?"

"That flyer!" I said. "The rally. She could tell whatever it was to someone in that association and they would tell the A.G."

"We still don't know what she knew. If anything. It could have been just an idle threat."

We were silent for a few moments. Staring out the windshield at the *Rex*'s lights in the distance. Back to work. "We interviewed Momma Margery and the Commodore. You did Andres, Miss Doone and all the people in the card game. Are we doing the doc next?"

"You don't want to have a *tete-a-tete* with Stanley?" He gave me a sideways glance, a twinkle in his eye, I thought.

I choked on that. Before I could reply, he said, "That's all right. Captain Ladd is doing the honors. If we're not satisfied with what he finds out, we can always go back to talk to Stanley and Ed. I can't see either of them doing her in and losing their nightly bath shows. They're peepers, not doers. What do you think, Graham?"

I thought about the squeaky window opening to announce, then reveal Venus on the half shell of her porcelain tub. I nodded.

If Marlowe wanted me to be surprised—shocked is a better word—he succeeded. He had arranged for the interview with the doc—to be at Kirsta's cottage.

A little macabre. Can't imagine what the doc thought. Next we'd be in the bathroom clustered around the tub.

Marlowe started off leisurely talking about Momma and the studio days when the doc worked there. We sat around the newspaper-covered coffee table.

Me on one of the two arm chairs. Marlowe at one end of the sofa, the doc at the other. Nothing matched, just beach cottage furniture, obviously a place rented out every year. It wasn't bad, a few brightly colored afghans took your eye away from the mismatch. All serviceable. But who was I to judge décor?

I had pen and pad ready but the doc was telling so many stories about their studio days, with Marlowe encouraging him by reminding him of tidbits of gossip. Just a good ol' boy fest. I might have felt exasperated, jumped up and down in frustration, but I knew Marlowe. Everything he did had a purpose. He wasn't just reminiscing for the fun of it.

Finally, Marlowe pulled a business card out of his shirt pocket and handed it to the doc saying, "Tell me about this. You're with the group that gives these out."

I strained to see what was on the card. Something about gambling. The doc didn't take the card, just glanced at it. Suddenly, he wasn't as animated as he had been when telling studio stories.

"It's a group that helps gamblers. Like AA for alcoholics. They offer help to people who want to quit." His voice was getting louder and higher. This was a subject he could go on about standing on a soap box. Just my impression.

I was ready to write down what he said. His gaze was fixed on Marlowe, waiting for the next question—or a punch to the gut, which is what his expression looked like he was expecting. In this case it would be a verbal punch.

Marlowe leaned forward and lifted a newspaper, revealing the flyer. I knew it was a copy because the original was being examined for fingerprints.

"Know anything about this?" Marlowe handed him the flyer. This time the doc took the item.

"It's what it says it is—a rally with the Attorney General to build support for closing down off-shore gambling."

Marlowe rubbed his chin.

The doc handed the flyer back to Marlowe. When Marlowe didn't reach for it, he dropped it on top of the newspapers.

"Tell me about this gambling disease. It's like alcoholism, you say?"

Yes, he had said all of that.

The doc answered perfunctorily, but Marlowe kept at it. He wanted to know more.

Finally, the floodgates opened and the doc talked about the compulsion, how the families were affected. Medically, the person couldn't be treated like an alcoholic or a drug addict, but they could be helped. Taking away dens of inequity like the *Rex* would be a big step in that direction.

He was passionate, filled with fervor, mentioned evil a few times. I expected some quotes from the Bible but that didn't come about.

I still didn't see where Marlowe was headed. So the guy wanted to save gamblers from themselves.

"Closing down the *Rex* will put you out of a job," Marlowe said.

"Ah, well, yes." The doc didn't say anything more.

"Will you go back to the studios?"

"No, probably get on staff at one of the hospitals."

"Perhaps where your wife died?"

Silence.

I gasped mentally. I sensed something coming.

"Yes," the doc finally answered.

Marlowe was asking questions but he could have been making statements. He knew the answers.

The doc nodded, taking his arm off the back of the sofa.

"Tell me about her," Marlowe said gently.

Tears came to the doc's eyes. "She was one of the addicts. Couldn't stay away from gambling." A sob shook him. "Started selling our furniture. Can't put someone like that anywhere to dry out. Gambling's an addiction but there was no place I could get help for her. She was…." Another sob "…desperate for money on the *Rex*. The Commodore called me. I wasn't working there then, but he knew I was Edna's husband." Sob. "It had come to the point…where…she was trying to sell herself." He choked the words out. "The Commodore locked her in one of the private rooms with a bodyguard. She broke a glass and cut her wrists before the bodyguard could stop her. Got her to the hospital in time. During the night she opened the wounds and bled to death." He mopped up a bit with his handkerchief.

"It was too late for her, but you can help others," Marlow said, still in a gentle voice.

"I've been trying. Some haven't come back, but there are always new ones. I can see it in their faces if they're addicts or not. Gambleritis. Those are the ones I'd like to save."

"The Commodore got you the job?"

"To work off her debt. He pays well. Plus he doesn't want another suicide attempt onboard. It's a big arrow in the Attorney General's quiver."

We were quiet for a while. I was digesting all this. Could see how the doc was of value to the Commodore, and why he'd hired him.

"How has it been? Have you lost anybody?"

"One man jumped overboard. We rescued him. Got him help. He's doing all right."

"But that's just one. If the Attorney General closes down the *Rex*, a lot more will be saved?"

"I hope so," the doc said in a whisper, like a prayer.

"Kirsta knew about the work you were doing for the Attorney General?"

"Work? What do you mean?"

"That you were working to close the *Rex* down?"

I think I gasped out loud this time because the doc looked at me. I quickly became absorbed in the squiggles I was making on the pad.

"That's ludicrous. I wouldn't be able to close the *Rex* down."

"All the information you gave the AG helps."

"What do you mean 'information'?"

"Insider information. Who goes there, who gambles too much and beyond their means, who the 'addicts' are, who's in debt to the Commodore. They've used that and will continue to use everything you give them."

"I'm not in that business. I'm just a doctor."

"You've witnessed more than one suicide attempt on the *Rex*, along with an attempt on the Commodore's life."

So Marlowe had learned a lot while I had been flatfooting on my beat around Hollywood.

"I can't talk about any of that. It's confidential medical information."

During this verbal tennis match, the doc had been shifting around on the sofa, not major moves, but enough to show that he wasn't comfortable with the questioning.

"Kirsta knew all this. Since she couldn't get money from the Commodore for the picture, she hit you up."

"I don't have any money."

"But she kept insisting."

"She didn't believe me when I told her I was broke. She kept saying I had to get the money. I kept asking her where was I going to get it from."

"She was going to tell the Commodore you were a spy for the AG."

"I just couldn't convince her how foolish that would be. I had no money, I was paying Edna's debt."

"If the Commodore even suspected what you were doing, you'd be food for the fishes."

More like pieces of him would have been fed to the fishes, bit by bit, while he was still alive, I thought.

"You had to keep her from telling him."

The doc said nothing. Now he was leaning forward. His hands clasped together between his knees. A picture of desolation.

"The same drug you gave Miss Doone?"

The doc sighed.

"It started off with you agreeing to help Momma and Kirsta in their campaign against Miss Doone," Marlowe stated. "Kirsta hinted about what she would do if you didn't help them."

The doc didn't move for a few minutes it seemed. Then he nodded.

Marlowe straightened up. He was on the scent, getting what he wanted.

"That's how she was blackmailing you. You probably called the Studio with the tip about Miss Doone. You didn't want Miss Doone to be found in a bad light. That tip brought me on the case. That was your one good deed. Only things went awry. Kirsta had the fight with the Commodore. She expected to get the money from him. And when she didn't, you were the next best choice."

"Margery knew I didn't have any money, but she wasn't around to tell Kirsta that. Kirsta was ready to call the Commodore to tell him everything. She was out of control, yelling, throwing things. I had to promise I would try. I told her I'd give her a little something so she'd feel better. She thought I was going to give her a shot of heroin. I let her think that. But it was a sedative. Something to put her to sleep for several hours. I had to talk to Margery so she could convince Kirsta not to do anything. Anything to calm her down, buy a little time."

"You didn't leave right away," Marlowe said. "You put her in the bathtub with a big ice cube that weighed twenty-five pounds from the icebox. You knew that hypothermia would do it. And who would know, the ice would be melted by the time anyone found her."

The doc didn't seem to be listening, he was still telling his story. "She was hysterical. She wouldn't listen to reason. I couldn't calm her down. I never saw her like that."

He suddenly looked at Marlowe. "Wait. What's this about ice? I gave her a sedative. She was out, here on the sofa in her robe. I covered her up with that afghan. She wouldn't wake up until morning. Then she might have taken a bath. How could she have died from hypothermia? The water wouldn't get that cold." He stopped and stared at Marlowe. "The block of ice? Why would she do that?"

Marlowe sat a little straighter. "She didn't. She was put in the bath by her murderer."

"Murderer? Kirsta was murdered?"

"Someone took the block of ice from the icebox and put it in the tub so she'd be sure to die."

"The last I saw of her she was in her robe asleep on this sofa." He stood up then got down on his hands and knees looking underneath. "And here are her shoes where she kicked them off."

Back to square one.

I think Marlowe had him pegged for the murder. Now he looked—well, puzzled. But more than that. Something else. What? As though he was trying to remember something. "Who would want to kill her?" Marlowe asked the doc.

The doc glanced at the flyer then picked it up. "Who wrote this?"

"You didn't because it doesn't match your handwriting. We thought maybe you had some else write it for you."

The doc shook his head.

Marlowe asked, "What's your best guess?"

The doc took his time, like he didn't want to squeal on anybody. He turned the sheet over. "Usually we address and mail them. No envelope. This may have been hand delivered. I know it's a copy."

"Nothing on the back of the original," Marlowe said.

"At the office," he said slowly, "there are a couple of boys, young men actually, who'd became her slaves, acolytes, however you want to describe them."

"Boys?"

"Young men, maybe twenty, if that. They look young. People are looking younger and younger to me every year."

Marlowe nodded, as though in appreciation.

"Why aren't they in the service?" I asked. Seemed everyone wanted to join.

"Medical reasons, I suppose. They tried. Too young to go to the *Rex*, so they couldn't be twenty-one. They were always hanging around here."

I thought back to the pictures I'd found in the chocolate box. The young men and women. Maybe they weren't couples, just friends who spent time together.

As though reading my thoughts, Marlowe pulled some snapshots from his pocket just like a magician would a rabbit.

"Duplicates," he said to me when he saw my expression of surprise. I knew Captain Ladd had the chocolate box full of the originals.

He handed each to the doc to identify. I noticed there was a number on the back. Five altogether. I had my pen ready. Only squiggles on the pad so far.

The doc IDed almost everyone and I duly wrote their names down, checking with him on the spelling. Derrick was one, Ronnie the other of the two boys.

"They all live around here, in the cottages. Don't know exactly where. Don't even know their last names. The boys volunteer at the office, so their addresses will be there."

"Will you get them for us?" Marlowe asked.

"Of course."

"Tell me about the boys," Marlowe said.

"They write scripts which they want to sell to Hollywood. Kirsta encouraged them. Told them she'd help. But they had to do things for her. In my view, she did everything she could to humiliate them, yet they kept doing whatever she asked. That was the price they were willing to pay."

Several thoughts raced through my mind. Sex was one of them. Even though the boys in the pictures looked a little pimply and didn't have the allure of the Commodore by any stretch of the imagination.

"Would they have killed her?" Marlowe asked.

Was he asking the fox to tell what happened in the henhouse? Now was the doc's opportunity to shift the suspicion onto them.

He thought for a while. "She laughed at them behind their backs. To me. Told me what she really thought. I don't think she was going to turn in their script, unless it was something that would make her look good for bringing it to a studio head's attention. Don't think it was."

"What picture did she want financing for?" I asked.

"An epic. That picture is already in the works and Miss Doone has the part. But Hollywood being Hollywood, if someone showed up with a fistful of dollars and said Kirsta had to be the lead, then she would be. She knew that. She knew the politics of Hollywood very well."

"Why did someone want Kirsta to go to the rally?" I asked.

"Her name. If she supported the group and the Attorney General, it would help them. She wasn't interested in politics, except studio politics. As long as things were going well with the Commodore, she wouldn't want to do anything to harm the *Rex*. But when that changed…" he splayed his hands in a gesture that implied 'anything could happen.'

The doc made a call and got the boys' address. They lived together, two streets over in one of the cottages.

Marlowe let the doc go home. We walked over to the cottage where the boys lived. I wondered if they were working at a paying job, as well as volunteering, or if one of them had a Daddy who paid the rent for the summer.

We climbed the two steps and opened the screen and wooden doors.

May the Lord spare me from ever having a boy like these two. Looked like an air bomb had gone off scattering everything. Clothes, papers everywhere, along with records stacked with and without their album covers.

I walked in then walked out. My mind couldn't handle such confusion. There could be bodies in there but no one would ever know. The smell was bad. Not dead body smell. Just locker room stench.

Marlowe let me off the hook. "Stay out here and talk to whoever comes by—about the boys."

Now I was sitting on the two steps at the front door. How can anyone, boys included, live like that?

It was 6 p.m. on a weekday so some people should be around, but there was no one except two little boys on tricycles using them like bumper cars crashing into each other.

Marlowe came out and lit a cigarette.

"Any dead bodies inside?"

"Nor live ones."

"I wondered what their script is about."

"Funny you should mention that. Here." He handed me a fat manila envelope addressed to Samuel Goldwyn. Only it had been returned. Unopened.

"Got nothing better to do. You going back in?"

He was pacing, smoking jerkily, like he couldn't pull the smoke into his lungs fast enough.

"Yep. Any luck with the passersby?"

"Just those two five-year-old delinquents on tricycles."

"Gotta train them early so you'll always have a job on the force." He went back in still smoking the cig.

I pretended I was Samuel Goldwyn, tore open the envelope, pulled out the pages and started reading. Reading scripts requires imagination, not something I have a lot of. But I didn't need any. It was the script Marlowe had told me about—movie star, two aspiring movie writers, blah blah blah, movie wins an Academy Award. Write what you know. At least they knew the first part of the story.

I kept glancing up, watching for the two inhabitants of the cottage. Then back to reading through the pages I'd scanned. If you're going to dream, might as well do it big. Suddenly I saw them down the narrow street. "Marlowe, I think they're here." I jumped up, opened the screen door and tossed the script in. I heard Marlowe exiting out of the back door. I closed both the screen and front doors and went to the side of the house where Marlowe was lighting another cigarette.

"Want one, Graham? We'll look more natural."

"Like we're not housebreaking? Are we going to interview them?"

He nodded.

Then boys appeared on the walkway in front. I recognized them from Kirsta's chocolate box photos.

"Derrick?" Marlowe said as we went toward them.

They looked startled, but not afraid. Wary. Not guilty looking. Not psychopaths like Leopold and Loeb.

"We want to talk to you about your script."

"Which one?" Derrick asked.

"The one that Kirsta Black had been showing round."

Did Marlowe just make that up?

They looked at each other. Now a bunch of emotions showed.

"Yeah, what about it?"

"I'm working for the studios—"

"You're lying. She said everyone said it was a piece of junk and that no one wanted to see any scripts from us ever again. She wasn't going to ruin her reputation by showing our sophomoric drivel to anyone." Ronnie mimicked her whiney voice.

"That's exactly what she said," Derrick said.

"Is that when you put her in the tub?"

The boys looked at each other.

Then they ran.

Marlowe pulled out another cigarette and chain lit it. "I guess that answers my question."

"Maybe they're working on a script titled *How to Kill a Movie Star*."

"How about *Murder At The Beach?*"

So the answer wasn't on the *Rex* after all. It was right here a few cottages away. The briny air smelled good, made me want to live at the beach. But I still needed a jacket.

"Now what?" I asked Marlowe.

"If you stay here, make sure they don't go inside to destroy the evidence, I'll find a telephone and tell Captain Ladd."

I thought more about titles. *Fade to Black* seemed like a good one.

I thought about Kirsta's disappointment in not getting money backing, and the Commodore's dismissal of her.

My take was that the boys had believed in her, pinned their hopes and dreams on her selling their script. They thought Kirsta Black was going to bat for them. It was about seeing their script on the big screen. Then all that was dashed with her tirade. They couldn't believe that she had lied to them, used them, and, in their opinion, made fools of them. Worse, in their minds probably.

The next day at Mom's Kitchen, Marlowe told me Captain Ladd had brought the boys in for a little serious talk. The boys said it was a prank, putting her into the tub. She had passed out while talking to them about their script. She'd been drinking.

Yes, they'd put her into the tub. Yes, they'd taken off her robe. No, they hadn't done anything else—they were gentleman after all. Then they thought about the block of ice. They pictured her coming to all cold, shivering, uncomfortable. That was the prank.

Captain Ladd also had a serious talk with the doc who had blown away the boys' statement when he told the rest of his story. After he had given Kirsta the sedative and she was out on the sofa, the boys had come by wanting to talk to her. The doc had told them she wasn't feeling well. Too much to drink. And told them about the sedative so they wouldn't come back to try to talk to her.

Marlowe quoted him. "They were drunk too, and mad. Good thing she wasn't awake. They looked mad enough to…"

Kill.

The boys knew about the sedative. They knew she wasn't going to wake up soon. So they put her in the tub with the ice. It was their word against the doc's. A little more questioning by Captain Ladd, and probably with Marlowe's help, Derrick revealed their hatred of the 'bitch.' Lots of other flavorful words, which Marlowe didn't relate to me, only alluded to, showed the depth of that hatred.

The boys had lied. It was no prank.

It was murder.

~The End~

Made in the USA
Columbia, SC
21 August 2023